A Step Back

A Step Back

Peter J. Wetzelaer and
Barbara A. Johnson

iUniverse, Inc.
Bloomington

A Step Back

iUniverse books may be ordered through booksellers or by contacting:

iUniverse
1663 Liberty Drive
Bloomington, IN 47403
www.iuniverse.com
1-800-Authors (1 800-288-4677)

ISBN: 978-1-4620-3893-0 (sc)
ISBN: 978-1-4620-3892-3 (hc)
ISBN: 978-1-4620-4041-4 (ebk)

Library of Congress Control Number: 2011912171

Printed in the United States of America

iUniverse rev. date: 07/22/2011

Dedication

Barbara A. Johnson and Peter J. Wetzelaer would like
to dedicate this novel to our deceased spouses.
Judith Wetzelaer and Richard Johnson.

Acknowledgments

We would like to thank Donna Lozy, Bob Bibeau,
and Linda Bird for reading our manuscript and
offering meaningful suggestions.

A violent thunderstorm ripped through the Yucatan Peninsula. A clap of thunder spooked a flock of keel-billed toucans, and without warning, a bolt of lightning struck and shattered the branch of a pink trumpet tree. A frightening black hue filled the skies as heavy rain soaked the region and strong winds forced the trees to bend to the near-breaking point as animals and birds scrambled for shelter. The deluge continued for fifteen minutes and then slowly came to a drizzle before stopping.

Gradually, the skies cleared and the sun enlightened the small Mayan village of Kukucan. In Mayan mythology, Kukucan means the wind god. More than three thousand years earlier, the Olmec and their descendents, the Mayans, lived in all parts of Mexico, Central and South America—known as Mesoamerica. The residents of Kukucan are direct descendants of these proud, ancient civilizations.

The early Mayans were primitive by today's standards, but they understood mathematics, physics, and astronomy. They knew the number zero was an important component in the science of numbers and arithmetic.

Present-day Kukucan had an area of five square miles surrounded by a forest and fields for growing crops; flowing to the east was the Maya river. The village was near the gulf, which generated a gentle breeze that kept the village at a comfortable temperature. Except for the occasional downpours or coastal storms, the sunshine was ceaseless. The several villages situated within Kukucan had a total population of 2,122.

A crowd of people, mostly women and children, were gathered outside the clinic, hoping to see a doctor. They had limited resources, and volunteer doctors looked after the medical needs of the people.

Kukucan's streets, except the main street, were dirt. A short distance from the center of the village, there was a structure they called the sanctuary, or meetinghouse, which was half the size of a football field. It had a thatched roof supported by long poles and a three-foot hay-and-reed wall surrounding the perimeter. There were openings in the wall for entering.

They observed special events, weddings, and funerals inside the meetinghouse. In the center, an altar was covered by a bright red cloth, various sized candles, and ancient ornaments. Open on all sides, a nice breeze kept the interior at a comfortable temperature.

A stone temple built hundreds of years earlier was situated fifty yards from the meetinghouse. It was eighty feet long by forty feet wide and rose to forty-seven feet. It was a testament to past Mayan construction projects and was the only evidence of ancient existence in the village.

Away from the center of the village, Anna Maria, aged eight, was sprinting, trying to avoid the puddles left from the thunderstorm. Hanging vines, vegetation, and brush covered both sides of the path.

She wore a rose-pink blouse and plaid red skirt with black sandals. She had long black hair, brown eyes, and a garland of flowers around her neck. Her pet donkey, Amigo, was moving at a quick gallop, trying to catch up.

Several years earlier, Maria had been picking flowers in the forest. A ground mist had been slowly dissipating into the atmosphere. While moving the brush, she noticed a baby donkey on a bed of leaves. The donkey did not move while he stared at Maria. He was thin and appeared to be sick and very drowsy.

She looked for his mother, but the little animal appeared to be alone. The colt was dun-grey with a white stripe between his eyes and stretching to his nose. She helped him to his feet, but his legs were weak and unstable. She cautiously led him home. The donkey was too weak to offer any resistance.

Maria was an expert and convinced her parents to keep the donkey. She took good care of her new friend and nursed him back to health. He grew quickly and, after several years, he weighed over four hundred pounds. She named him Amigo, and they became inseparable. Acting like a dog, he would follow her wherever she went.

As Maria rounded a curve in the pathway, a hand grabbed her arm.

"Ouch! That hurt," she said as she examined the bruise on her upper limb.

"Where is your father?" a stern voice asked.

Terrified, Anna Maria noticed that three men had come out of the bushes.

"Why do you want to see him?" she asked.

"It's business. We are his friends, and we won't harm him."

"I know all of my father's friends, and I don't know you," she said.

"Little one, I suggest you take us to him—now!"

Chapter 2

The chief of the village, Pochotl Toltec, was better known as Paco. With hands crossed and head bowed, he stood in front of the altar to pay respect to his ancestors.

When his father was unable to perform his duties, the oldest son assumed the position of chief. This had been the Mayan tradition for many years.

Paco wore a white shirt, white pants, and a straw hat that hung low on his back. At thirty-six, he was almost six feet and had a thin build. He was clean-shaven, but he could use a haircut. His family consisted of a wife, Rosa, two daughters—Anna Maria and Angela—and a baby son, Luis.

To support his family, he grew vegetables and fruits and raised a few turkeys and chickens. Occasionally, he fished in the ocean or harvested shellfish.

Solving problems was part of Paco's duties as chief. Crimes were rare, as children learned at an early age to exercise good conduct. Tending to chores, studying at school, and participating in physical games kept their minds occupied. Punishments were not pleasant since dishonor would come to their families if they violated any Mayan rules. A strong commitment to Mayan traditions and family values kept the village in harmony.

They governed themselves as a sovereign nation. The people were hardworking, peaceful, and shy. Paco and the other residents of Kukucan took part in a crop-growing system called *milpa*. In Spanish, *milpa* means field. The system was very simple. They grew crops for two years, and then they would plow for eight years and leave the fields dormant. Rotating the crops, there was no need for fertilizers or pesticides. This agricultural method, used for thousands of years, produced large yields of crops.

They would sell their surplus crops to neighboring villages and larger cities. The villagers of Kukucan would share the income to pay for electrical necessities and other conveniences of the modern world. The Mayans of Kukucan had harvested and occupied the land for thousands of years.

Homes were made of cinderblock and stone. Corrugated metal and thatched hay were used for the roofs. Grass lawns and colorful landscaping were missing; rusted washtubs, stripped cars, and various other junk littered the yards. The village had a few stores, a clinic, and a butcher shop—it was enough to fill the limited needs of the inhabitants. Most homes had electrical power, and several dwellings had TV and satellite dishes. Vintage automobiles that required major bodywork were parked in yards and streets. It was doubtful that any were in running condition.

Anna Maria entered the sanctuary with Amigo and the three men from the pathway. She was a precocious little girl who loved her environment. Every chance she got, she would take trips to the forest to pick flowers and observe the animals. She knew and avoided the dangers lurking in the wilderness. She was called Maria in honor of her grandmother.

"Papa, these men would like to talk to you. They say they are your friends."

Paco turned abruptly and recognized the outlaw Miguel Ramirez. Miguel was barely five foot five and was a little overweight. He wore rattlesnake boots, denim jeans, and a Panama-style shirt. His black curly hair matched his unshaven face. A cigar was dangling from his lip, and he barely opened his mouth when he spoke.

"Yes, they are," Paco said. "Maria, take Amigo home. I think he's hungry."

She ran to her father, kissed him, and then took Amigo with her.

Miguel said, "Paco, have all the arrangements been made?"

"Yes," said Paco. "The submarine arrived yesterday and is out of sight. The product has been processed and taken to a safe place."

"Excellent," said Miguel. "In three days, I want you to deliver the product to the submarine. Tell your people to be extra careful while loading the cargo. If anything goes wrong, I will not be happy! Do you remember the first day we entered this village? I'm sure you don't want a repeat of a very unpleasant situation."

Paco said, "Don't worry—they will be attentive. Our strongest men will load the cargo."

"Fine . . . and remember what I told you."

When the three men left the sanctuary, Paco remembered a story his grandfather had told him many years earlier. In the fifteenth century, the Aztec emperor, Montezuma, turned over his kingdom to Hernan Cortez, the Spanish explorer. Montezuma had hundreds of warriors in his population and thought Cortez was a god. Cortez had less than a hundred men in his group, but was able to conquer Montezuma's kingdom.

The Aztecs finally figured out what was happening and fought the Spanish. While trying to defend his kingdom, Montezuma was killed by the Spanish during one of many battles.

If only his village had the courage to rise up. Paco knew Miguel Ramirez was violent and would wipe out his village if he detected any dissent. Everyone was too afraid to do anything except what Miguel told them.

Chapter 3

The sun was peeking over the horizon. It was a new day in the nation's capital. It was partly cloudy, and the temperatures were near forty. An alarm sounded loudly and danced around the night table. Ray Callahan reached over and quieted the vibration.

His wife was already out of bed, buttering a piece of toast.

"What do you want for breakfast?" she asked.

"Just yogurt," he replied.

She handed him a yogurt and a spoon. When he was done, he brushed his teeth and put on his jogging clothes.

He asked, "What's going on today?"

Lori replied, "Just correcting midterms and meeting some parents." Lori was twenty-five and five foot seven and had a statuesque look. Her long brunette hair went well with her slim figure thanks to the gym she used at the academy.

"Sounds good, hon." He finished tying his running shoes and kissed her. "See you tonight," he said as he rushed out the door.

Nearing thirty, Ray was in better-than-average shape. He was six foot four, and his lengthy brown hair sometimes obstructed his view when he jogged.

Ray and Lori lived in a two-bedroom apartment in the heart of Washington. They had moved into the third floor of an eleven-floor apartment building when they married, making it their first home. The apartment had a modern kitchen; it was small, but cozy. There was a good-sized living room with a large picture window overlooking the main street. Their contemporary bathroom had a walk-in shower instead of a tub. Ray loved the water pressure and the clean feel of his body.

Lori decorated the apartment with knick-knacks, pictures, flowers, and all the little things that make an apartment a home. Attached to the apartment building was a parking garage where residents had assigned parking spaces. It was gated, secure, and in a good neighborhood.

Ray took the elevator down to the first floor. As he got off, he narrowly missed colliding with Mrs. Bouthiette. She was on her way out to take her dog for a walk. He said hello, and she nodded as he trotted out the front entrance.

Along the tree-lined street, specialty shops, stores, and restaurants occupied the first floor of the buildings. Jackhammers and construction equipment caused an irritating noise on the busy roadway. The crew was repairing a cracked water main. The water level was not high, and they were desperately trying to avoid a major break. Ray tried to go around the traffic. A taxi almost hit him; the driver yelled at him in a language that he did not understand.

When he entered his favorite coffee shop, Maxwell was already holding his preferred blend of latte. Ray and Maxwell had become good friends when they discovered that they both had served in the army.

"That's $2.50," said Maxwell.

"I don't have any money, I'm in my jogging clothes," said Ray as he grabbed the coffee from Maxwell's hand.

"He does this every day," Maxwell said to a coworker, "but he always settles at the end of the month."

When Ray reached his building, Mrs. Bouthiette was still walking her dog. Kellie, a beautiful two-year-old German Shepherd, was smart, strong, and affectionate. Lori had already left for work. As he was drying himself off from a hot shower, the phone rang.

Jim Mathews, a fellow agent said, "The boss would like to see us at ten o'clock in his office."

"Okay," I'll be there."

Ray finished dressing and started his short journey to his office.

Chapter 4

Ray pulled up to his office building and could see the dome of the Capitol flickering in his rearview mirror.

The front entrance to his building had large double wooden doors. The white sandstone building was impressive. No one used this entrance because most people used the parking garage connected to the building. The grounds had been recently mowed and were nicely landscaped. Any indication or signs to identify the facility were absent.

As he pulled into the parking garage, a stop bar blocked his way. Bill Arnold and Ed McNally, the security guards, approached. Bill and Ed had worked as police officers in New England. When they discovered that Ray came from Boston, they all became friends.

Bill asked, "Where's your badge, Ray?"

"Bill, you do this to me every day. You know me."

"Ray, you know the rules. Nobody gets in without a badge."

Ray fumbled around, found the badge, and showed it to Bill.

"Okay," said Bill. "Pull it on—you're going to need it inside. See you Saturday morning on the first tee."

Ray waved as he pulled into the garage. He locked his car and walked to the third-floor entrance. Another security guard was sitting on a wooden stool. Benny allowed Ray to enter after he showed his badge. Ray swiped his badge across the machine that would log him into the facility. He placed his thumb on a surface that recorded his print. When completed accurately, a green light illuminated. It resembled a time clock, but was much more advanced. He used the same procedure when he left the facility.

Ray walked to his cubicle and checked his memos and e-mail. A Red Sox baseball schedule hung on the wall. His cubicle included pictures of Lori and his parents. His father was a Boston police officer whose beat was the neighborhood around Fenway Park. His mother was an emergency room nurse at Beth Israel Hospital. Thirty three years earlier, they had met when his father was shot during a robbery attempt. His mother treated the wound, and the rest was history. Ray and his family grew up with a strong commitment to the community.

Ray felt homesick when thinking of St. Brigid's Parish, the basketball games, his friends the T, and dinner at Durgin Park.

"Hi, Ray." Jim Mathews leaned over the divider from the next cubicle. "Ready to see the boss?"

"Yup," said Ray with a smile, but showed a little concern.

Jim Mathews was an agent from Torrance, California. He was active in sports and had worked as a lifeguard. After high school, he enlisted in the navy and eventually became a Seal. When his enlistment ended after six years, he attended UCLA. Jim was single, in excellent shape, and good looking. He lived several blocks from Ray's neighborhood. He had relationships with several women, but nothing serious.

Jim joined Ray in his cubicle. They were chewing the fat when Barbara West joined them. She was blonde and had an outstanding figure. Her pink shirt and black miniskirt added to her beauty. The black high heels emphasized her legs.

Barbara worked for Betty Jordan, Bob Miller's executive secretary.

She offered to get them coffee and headed for the pantry.

"What's up with the meeting?" asked Ray.

"Damned if I know," said Jim. "They usually don't tell you until you get to the meeting."

When Barbara returned with two black coffees, she placed one in front of Ray. When she handed Jim his coffee, they looked longingly into each other's eyes. She looked at her watch and said, "Time to go—see you later."

Ray and Jim waved as she left.

Ray was scanning some papers when Lori called to tell him that they had been invited to dinner with friends. The Cunninghams had been instrumental in getting Ray and Lori their positions. When they graduated from college, Russ and Chris convinced them to move to Washington and assisted them in finding their current careers.

Jim leaned over his cubicle to tell Ray it was time to meet with the boss.

Chapter 5

B ob Miller supervised a group of special agents, law professionals, and support personnel. Betty Jordan's desk was located in the front vestibule leading to the meeting room. As Ray and Jim approached, Betty looked up and asked, "Did Barbara take care of you boys this morning?"

"Oh yes," said Jim as he glanced over at Barbara.

She looked up from the copy machine, smiled, and then returned to work.

Betty had been with the company for eighteen years. She knew her business and ran a tight ship.

"Mr. Miller is waiting for you. Go right in."

Bob had worked for the company for twenty-nine years. He was eight months from retirement.

Bob said, "This is Franco Villa from the Mexican consulate. Ray, Most of your cases in the past six months have been routine. We think you're ready for something more challenging. I need men with your experience for an upcoming project. I'll let Mr. Villa continue."

Villa walked to a map on the wall showing the southern parts of the US, the Yucatan Peninsula, and most of the islands in the Caribbean and Gulf. He pointed to a section of the Yucatan and said, "This is Kukucan. It has come to our attention that Miguel Ramirez is conducting illegal business there. Since Kukucan is a sovereign Mayan nation, the government of Mexico has no jurisdiction. There is a treaty that dates back many hundreds of years. The politicians know what's going on, but their hands are tied.

"Ramirez and his cartel bring contraband to the village to be processed, and later it is hidden somewhere in the forest. When the illicit goods are ready for shipment, they load it onto a one-man submarine. This operation covers several nations and is a multimillion-dollar enterprise.

"Gentleman, the United States and Mexico have a mutual legal assistance treaty, and my country needs your help."

Bob Miller said, "Our sources tell us a special fiberglass was used in the construction of the sub. It is small and difficult for radar and sonar to detect. It has the capability to emit sounds that resemble large fish and whales. At times, it travels under cruise ships to avoid detection."

"Is this information reliable?" asked Ray.

"This information comes from sources we cannot divulge," Bob said. "This is a covert operation. You are on your own. Take a radio and notify us when the mission is complete. I want you both to go to Kukucan and destroy that sub."

"Won't they just build another sub?" asked Jim.

"Then we'll blow that one up too," said Bob.

Chapter 6

The mighty Hercules C-130 banked to avoid Mexican airspace. The four-engine turboprop was cruising in the Gulf of Mexico five miles from Kukucan. As the plane reduced altitude to 1,100 feet, the large rear-loading platform opened and Ray and Jim departed the aircraft.

During the freefall, they located the outline of the drop zone they were looking for. The full moon illuminated the landing area. They had a long glide as they deployed their ram-air canopy. They turned and flared to their destination.

They buried the parachutes and satellite radio in an isolated area at the edge of the forest. They loaded the explosives, weapons, and other needed materials into backpacks.

Villa had supplied a map of Kukucan and a photo of Paco. The map outlined the dock, clinic, and Paco's home.

It took a half hour to walk to Kukucan. They hid their backpacks in the forest on the opposite side of the Maya River. It was nearing midnight, and most of Kukucan was quiet. Ray and Jim swam across the Maya river and found Paco's home.

A frightened Paco answered the knock on his door. The intrusion did not awaken the rest of his family.

Ray and Jim identified themselves and described their reason for waking him. Paco was grateful that help had finally arrived. He mentioned that they were loading the cargo in the morning and it would be a month before they had another opportunity to destroy the sub. They thanked Paco for the information and told him that they would keep in touch.

When they saw that the sub was out of hiding and tied to the dock, they retrieved their hidden equipment. The lightweight Closed Circuit Underwater Breathing Apparatus was a closed system that did not produce any bubbles.

Jim examined the photo that and said, "Ray, look at this photo."

Ray looked at the photo and then looked at the sub.

"It's not the same," he said.

"You're right. The photo is a picture of a semi-submersible used by the drug cartel in Columbia. What we are looking at is a World War II German Bieber miniature submarine. When I was in the navy, I did a lot of research on submarines . . . it was sort of a hobby. During the war, the Germans built over three hundred of these little submarines. They could lay mines and carry two torpedoes attached to each side. They had a thirteen-horsepower electric motor when submerged. Their speed was slow according to today's standards—only 5.3 knots submerged and 6.5 knots on the surface. For surface propulsion, they used an Otto petrol engine that had a nasty reputation of expelling deadly carbon monoxide. It killed many of the pilots."

"What's that sub doing here?" asked Ray.

"The drug cartels have a great deal of cash. Their influence is far reaching. I can see they have reinforced the hull so they can go deeper—maybe a hundred feet. They have added sonar and a GPS system. I bet they changed the Otto engine for something modern and updated the propeller blades for greater speed. It wouldn't surprise me if they have the ability to stay submerged longer."

They swam out to the sub and started to mold the C-4 explosives around the hull. The plastic material held the detonators.

At daybreak, the strongest men were loading the cargo onto the submarine. Miguel had armed guards patrolling the loading area.

The skies had darkened as a threat of rain was looming.

Both sides of the sub were concave. This allowed the torpedoes to fit snugly along the side of the vessel. Plastic tubes, twenty-one inches in diameter and twenty-five feet long, had the same dimensions as a torpedo. The plastic tubes held most of the contraband. The remainder was stored inside the sub.

They were strapped to both sides of the sub using the same method they used with torpedoes. If they were spotted out in the Gulf, the cargo was jettisoned and fell to the bottom of the ocean.

The dark-blue submarine was thirty feet long. A periscope was located in the center of the aluminum alloy conning tower and was bolted to the top. The conning tower's armored glass windows allowed the pilot to observe any outside activities. Depending on operating conditions, diesel or battery-powered electric motors propelled the sub. The pilot and only crewmember, Ramone, had extensive submarine experience with a foreign navy. He also had a long history of crime and violence.

Miguel was giving final instructions. "Follow the river to the ocean. Stay on the surface until the cruise ship leaves Cozumel. You know the ship's course—submerge and wait for the ship to pass over you. Stay with the ship until you reach Key West. Break away and surface. It'll be dark, but the southernmost marker should be illuminated. Call Jeff Longstreet and say, "Your pizza is ready." When Jeff arrives, his crew will load the cargo onto his boat. They will hoist both plastic tubes onto his vessel. Your job is finished when the transfer is completed."

Three years earlier, Jeff Longstreet's father had died, and he had inherited the tourist and airboat business. When the economy took a downturn, the tourist trade suffered. He was about to lose his company when he met Miguel. He was not pleased, but he worked with Miguel to save his business.

Once the contraband was in Key West, it was smuggled to the Florida mainland by airboats or tourist boats.

The loading at Kukucan was moving rapidly. Below the waterline and out of sight, Ray and Jim were finished attaching plastic explosives to the hull. They set the timers and swam to the far side of the river.

It wasn't long before the hatches closed. The sub slowly pulled away from the dock. Miguel, Tomas, and another associate were watching from a nearby hill. Miguel was smiling.

The sub headed for the ocean along the Maya River. The clouds had cleared as the morning grew brighter. When the sub was almost out of sight, it blew up.

Chapter 7

As the sub burned, a black cloud of smoke billowed high into the sky. The villagers watched as the smoke rose higher and higher into the heavens. They turned and ran for their homes. Mothers gathered their children, shutters and windows closed. The streets were quiet. They feared Miguel Ramirez.

Ramirez had grown up on the vicious streets of Mexico City. At fourteen, he quit school and left home. His knowledge of the streets helped him survive. He was not married, but had five children with three women—he never stayed in one place for very long.

Growing up, he'd had many run-ins with the law. He would drink too much and spend many nights in jail. He bullied, molested, and ridiculed most people he encountered. As he aged, his crimes became more violent. Robbery and murder put him in prison for a decade. When he got out, he started to work for a drug cartel and advanced to a high position. He was ruthless, but he became very successful and wealthy.

Paco was in the meetinghouse at the altar. His head was bowed—his hands crossed behind his back.

"Paco!"

Paco Turned abruptly. Anna Maria had a gun to her head.

Miguel, with hatred in his eyes, shouted, "You gave our secret to the federales. I told you if you did not cooperate with us, I would kill your people."

"Please don't harm my daughter!"

"After I kill everyone, I'm going to set fire and destroy your village!"

"No, no," cried Paco. "My daughter and people are innocent—they had nothing to do with telling the federales. I told them."

"Who is going to pay for all the money I lost?"

"Say your prayers, Paco. It's time to die." Miguel pointed the gun at Paco.

Suddenly, Jim and Ray appeared behind Miguel.

"Drop that gun," demanded Ray. Miguel froze, looked at Ray, and asked, "Are you the men who destroyed my business?"

"Your business had a lot of problems," Ray said.

Anna Maria ran to her father. He told her to go to her mother. She ran out of the sanctuary. As Anna Maria disappeared out of sight, a shot rang out. Jim Mathews groaned and fell to the floor. Two of Miguel's associates, holding guns, were standing on the far side of the sanctuary.

Ray turned, fired, and killed the outlaw who had shot Jim. The second outlaw ran into the forest and vanished. During the confusion, Miguel shot Ray. Just as Miguel was drawing closer, Jim, mortally wounded, shot and killed Miguel.

Ray passed out from his wound.

Chapter 8

The doctors at the clinic treated Ray's injuries. They removed the bullet and sterilized the wound. The bullet had missed vital organs; with rest, he would recover.

Jim's funeral took place in the meetinghouse. Spiritual members conducted a traditional Mayan ceremony. Ray did not attend since the outlaws were still looking for him. On a hill overlooking the Maya River, there was a burial service as Jim left for a better world.

Ramone was the son of Tomas, second in command to Miguel. He wanted to find Ray to get his revenge, but the villagers were successful in hiding him.

Tomas had chicken pox scars on his face. He wore a dirty sombrero, and many of his teeth were missing. He wore a crossed gun belt with bullets and pistols like the bandits of the Old West.

Four pickup trucks came roaring through the dusty streets. Dogs, geese, and chickens tried to escape the chaos. Men with rifles rode on the flatbeds. They came to a screeching halt in front of an abandoned garage. A stretch Hummer pulled up, and six men with automatic weapons jumped out. They looked around and motioned that he was okay. A man in his early thirties got out. They all went inside. Other gang members came from the forest to join them.

A makeshift lab operated in the garage. The finished contraband was packaged and concealed in the forest. Inside, they gathered around Luis, the kingpin of the cartel.

Luis removed his sunglasses and asked, "What's going on?"

Tomas said, "The sub was destroyed and Miguel was killed. The sub was blown up by two Americans—one of which we killed. Paco, the chief of the village, assisted the gringos, but our orders were not to harm him. We wanted to kill the American, but we cannot find him. We know the villagers are involved."

Luis said, "When we lost the sub and the cargo, the cartel lost a great deal of money. We are not in business to lose money. We selected this place because it was secret—well, it's no longer a secret. I fear that Mexican troops or even US Marines may come to protect these people. I am not putting any more money into this operation. We are looking for better places like Belize or Costa Rica. Pack up the lab—we are moving."

"Do we kill the people and level the village?" asked Tomas.

"No no! Leave these people alone. That's an order."

Tomas was confused and wanted to question the order, but he did not dare.

The men started to leave and join their vehicles. Luis was about to enter his Hummer when he noticed a figure across the street. Luis stopped and stared at Paco. Slowly, he put on his sunglasses, got into his vehicle, and gave the order to leave.

Luis was Paco's younger brother. He had been born and raised in Kukucan, but he had left when the quiet life and Mayan ways did not suit him. His early life was similar to Miguel's, but he was intelligent and had attended college. His neighbors in the big city had no knowledge of his real occupation. To them, he was a successful lawyer who was very generous to his family. He supported many charities and causes; he was a pillar of the community

Ray had become close to Paco during his recuperation. Ray had saved Anna Maria from Miguel's threats, and Paco wanted to repay him.

When Ray was well enough to travel, Paco brought him to a strange place. Rocks, vegetation, and the climb to the entrance were challenging. Relics from the Mayan and Olmec past surrounded the cave. An opening near the roof allowed sunlight to illuminate the interior.

Most of the village had knowledge of the cave, but the only visitors allowed were Paco, a few trusted elders, and some young volunteers who would periodically clear the vegetation and dust from the interior. Pea stone covered most of the floor and rock formations lined the walls.

Artifacts were placed on stone shelves or stored inside the large crevices.

Paco said that he was grateful for what Ray and Jim Mathews had done for him and his village. "I would like you to accept a gift from the people of Kukucan," he said.

"Your friendship is enough for me. A gift is not necessary."

Paco reached up to a hidden shelf. He brought down a circular relic that looked very odd. It was eighteen inches in diameter and three inches high. It was covered in Mayan symbols and decorative artwork. On top were five rings—each ring was independent. A silver medallion the size of a US half dollar was on top. The medallion cover had symbols of an unfamiliar source. At the outer edge was an eight-pointed diamond star. The point closest to the center was longest. Mayan numbers and values were displayed on each ring. The numbers looked like Morse code with dots and dashes. The difference was that the dashes were above the dots.

He handed the relic to Ray.

"It weighs about sixteen pounds," said Paco. "Mayan symbols were black and the main bodies were olive. Each dot had a value of one; the dash, a value of five. This device, a Veracruz, allows a person to travel back in time. For the time you wish to visit, adjust the five rings to set the time and date. Each ring functions as the year, month, day, hour, and minute. This is Mayan time—not Gregorian. Most Western nations use the Gregorian calendar.

"To set the rings to the desired date, you must use a conversion table. All rings begin at the origin point. Let me show you how it works. I use the star as a pointer, and I've adjusted the rings to represent a time fifty years ago. Place your thumb on the star and push until the compartment containing a bottle slides out. The silver medallion retracts, exposing the filler hole. Remove the Olmec potion and the top from the bottle. Carefully apply the required drops into the filler hole. You have one minute to apply the drops. When the minute has lapsed, the silver medallion will automatically cover the filler hole and the rings will return to their origin as the compartment closes. This feature is required to prevent the filler hole from remaining open, allowing debris to fall into the opening.

"Replace the top and put the bottle back in the compartment. Push the star until the compartment retracts and the silver medallion moves over the filler hole. Place a finger on the silver medallion. A mist will cover the Veracruz and engulf you. The mist turns into a slight breeze. The breeze is soft and gentle. It's called a Zephyr.

"You will observe everything that transpires, but no one can see or interact with you. You are just a breeze. The time length of the breeze is determined by the number of drops put into the filler hole. The Veracruz was given to our ancestors many years ago. Strangers from places unknown gave my people this gift. They were intelligent and traveled on round silver clouds. They also advised us when we built the temples and when our calendars were conceived. The Veracruz is not to be used to harm innocent people, for monetary or personnel gain, or—most importantly—for altering history."

"What would happen if I did any of these things?"

"You would always remain as a Zephyr and the results would be very unpleasant. I know that this information is complex, but it's very simple as you become familiar with the Veracruz. It's truly a special instrument as you will soon discover. Extraterrestrials may have assisted the Mayans in the construction of their pyramids and other advanced technologies. In ancient caves, there are Mayan stone sculptures that resemble aliens from other worlds."

Chapter 9

Paco and Ray were still in the cave.

"I'm anxious to try the Veracruz," said Ray.

"Very well. How far back in time do you want to go?"

"How about last night?"

"Okay, we'll go back to ten o'clock last night."

Paco's father had taught him the conversion principle between the Gregorian and Mayan calendars. He took a notebook and a pencil from his shirt pocket. He quickly calculated the required setting. He told Ray to get closer so that he could show him how to adjust the rings.

"I've already calculated the settings I need. See the diamond star on the outer edge? All the rings start at their origin position. I rotate the outer ring to match the Mayan symbol for the chosen year to the long pointer on the star. I do the same for the month, day, hour, and minute rings. It may sound complicated, but it's actually very simple. The hardest part is converting the Gregorian date to the Mayan equivalent. Later, I will teach you the method. What duration would you like?"

"What do you mean?"

"The number of drops in the filler hole will determine the time you spend at the chosen date. The first drop will yield a six-minute interval. The second drop will produce a factor of ten, which is an hour. The third drop will also produce a factor of ten, which is ten hours. Applying more than three drops is dangerous. You may never come back."

"Okay, I'm ready."

Ray stepped up to the Veracruz. Paco pushed the star. The compartment with the Olmec potion opened. He removed the top and applied one drop into the filler hole. He put the top back on the bottle and returned it to the compartment. He pushed the star; the compartment retracted and the silver medallion covered the filler hole.

He told Ray to place a finger on the silver medallion and Ray obeyed.

A mist surrounded the Veracruz and then the whole cave. Ray and the Veracruz vanished. The mist cleared to a slight breeze. A circle of dust danced on the floor. As the mist developed, all the Veracruz rings returned to their origin and every color vanished.

Soon the cave darkened. Stars filled the sky as a meteor shot pass the moon. The temperature cooled. After six minutes, Ray and the Veracruz returned.

Ray looked as if he had confronted a ghost. When the blood returned to his face, he said, "I saw it all. What a terrific experience. Did you see it too, Paco?"

"Even though I was part of the mist, I didn't take part in the observation with you. I remained at the current time. Only the person with their finger on the medallion can return to the past."

"Going back in time can be very dangerous. Do not tell anyone about your gift. Use the Olmec Potion sparingly. There are no refills. There may be a formula buried somewhere in the Mayan ruins, but it has never been found."

"Have your people used the Veracruz?"

"The Olmec and then the Mayans used it hundreds of years ago. Being a simple people, they soon tired of it. They tried to destroy the Veracruz. Some thought it was evil. They dropped rocks from great heights, but there was no damage. They burned it in bonfires for days and still failed to destroy it. The people determined it was a gift from the gods and put it away for safekeeping."

"How many more Veracruz devices are there?"

"Our village has one and it is well hidden. There are others in villages throughout the Mayan community, but they are hardly mentioned anymore."

"How does the Veracruz work?"

"The secret of the Veracruz left with the strangers."

Chapter 10

After the outlaws left, Ray was able to retrieve his radio. The batteries were weak, but he was able to contact the company.

He reported that the mission was successful and outlaws had killed Jim Mathews. He mentioned his wound. The company told him to report back in three hours.

He walked to Paco's home to charge the batteries. Paco was working, but his wife and children were home. While Ray played with the daughters, Rosa offered him something to eat. The Mayan women did not eat with the men.

After three hours, the batteries were charged. He went outside and contacted the company. The company told him to be ready to leave in two days. A fishing boat would pick him up at five in the morning on the Kukucan dock and take him to Cozumel. As Ray concluded his exchange, Paco approached from the meetinghouse. He told Paco he was leaving in a few days.

Paco was saddened that his friend was leaving, but understood that Ray missed his wife and wanted to return home. He arranged for a festival in Ray's honor.

The next day, the festival commenced at the meetinghouse. Mayan costumes and bright ornaments added to the festivities. There was music, dancing, and lots of food.

Amigo was there wearing his favorite straw hat, which he later ate.

When the festival concluded, Ray thanked the villagers. Anna Maria presented him with a bouquet of flowers. Paco hugged Ray as they said good-bye. Ray promised he would return to Kukucan.

Early the next morning, Kukucan was quiet. Ray was waiting on the dock. He had a duffel bag with his limited belongings. Paco had made a case that resembled a small footlocker—safely inside was the Veracruz.

Soon, a fishing boat approached and docked.

A heavyset man asked, "Are you Ray?"

Ray nodded.

"Come aboard. I'm Hugo." He introduced the two other crewmembers.

The boat was sixty-five feet long and powered by two inboard engines. The engines were unusually quiet. It had a galley and sleeping quarters. Mounted at the rear of the boat were various fishing poles and equipment, including radar and other electronic devices. Many radio antennas were installed, which seemed inappropriate for a fishing boat.

A crewman tended to fishing equipment while the other piloted the boat.

Hugo handed Ray a lifejacket. "Hope you won't need this," he said with a smile.

The sun was rising over the eastern portion of Cozumel Island as the boat pulled up to the dock. A black stretch limousine with tinted windows was waiting with its engine running. Ray thanked Hugo and waved to the other fishermen as he departed the boat.

The chauffeur put the duffel bag in the trunk and held the door as Ray entered. As Ray started to sit down, Franco Villa offered his hand. Villa thanked Ray on behalf of the people of Mexico. Jim's death came up. They talked more about the mission as they approached the airport.

Security guards waved the limo through the private gate and parked beside a jet. Ray introduced himself to the pilot and crew as he boarded the aircraft. He was treated as a VIP and a hero. Villa waved good-bye as the jet roared into the Yucatan airspace.

Chapter 11

A light snow was falling at Andrews Air Force base. Ray entered the terminal lobby and noticed Lori waving frantically trying to get his attention.

Ray rushed to her and gave her a passionate kiss. "I love you and missed you."

"I love you too."

They found their way to the parking lot. Ray slipped and almost fell due to the freezing weather.

"I hate the snow," she said.

Ray came from South Boston or Southie as it was called. The bad weather and snow was not a problem for him. Lori had grown up in Florida.

Lori and Ray met when they attended Bryant University in Rhode Island. When they finished college, they married and found positions in the Washington area. He went to work for the company while Lori found a teaching job in Alexandria.

As they were driving home, Lori said, "For six weeks, I didn't know what happened to you. The day you left, Betty Jordan called to say you were on assignment and it might be a while before I heard from you. Finally, your boss called. He didn't say much, but he did say you had been involved in a shooting and were going to be okay. I wish he hadn't told me that. I was a nervous wreck. Your job is too dangerous. What about your next assignment? I want you to quit your job."

When Ray reported back to the company, the medical people examined his wound and found it had healed. He desperately needed some time off, and he received it. He loved his job although he knew it was dangerous and was concerned that Lori was frightened about his next assignment. When she learned that Jim Mathews had died, her fears were reinforced.

Ray and Lori accepted a dinner invitation from the Cunninghams. When they arrived, Ray apologized for missing their last dinner engagement.

The Cunninghams lived in a luxury apartment across the street. The women were best friends from high school and had grown up in the same neighborhood and church.

Russ had an executive position in the company. He had graduated from Duke and had an MBA from Harvard.

Chris and Russ were childless. Chris was a part-time actress in a few high school, local, and amateur plays; she enjoyed the excitement of the theater, but did not want to perform professionally.

Ray was thankful to be back home and enjoyed spending time with Lori and the Cunninghams.

When the alarm sounded for Ray's first day back to work, he put on his jogging clothes. He kissed Lori and said, "See you tonight; I love you."

The sun was shining with a few puffy clouds moving slowly eastward. It was a crisp day.

When he arrived at the coffee shop, he asked, "Where's Maxwell?"

The young girl behind the counter replied, "Maxwell is not here yet; he's the manager and doesn't come in until later."

"I'm sorry I missed him. Can I have a latte?"

As Ray was waiting, Maxwell entered from the back room. "Well, well, what do we have here?"

"I came in to pay my bill."

Maxwell smiled. "Your bill has been paid."

"Who paid it?"

"I did. I wrote it off to Goodwill."

The girl handed Ray his latte.

"What do I owe you?"

"It's still on the Goodwill budget . . . nice seeing you, Ray."

When he arrived at work, the stop bar was down.

"Hi, stranger. Where's your badge?" said Bill.

"Oh no. Where's that badge?" Ray eventually found the badge. "Put it on, Ray. You're going to need it inside."

"How've you been, Bill?"

"Not bad, I waited for you at the first tee. It started to snow, so I went home."

"I'm sorry, you know how this business is."

"I know," Bill said as the stop bar started to lift.

When Ray reached his cubicle, he looked at Jim's empty cubicle. Someone had cleaned and removed all his belongings and pictures.

Ray exchanged welcome-back greetings from several of his coworkers and resumed his normal duties. He was working on a project when he got a call from Lori.

"Ray, it's snowing and the weather people say it's going to get worse. They sent all the students back to their dormitories. They closed the academy and wanted the teachers to go home. I'm on my way and I wish you would do the same. I'm not stopping, but can you pick up some bread, milk, and sandwich meat?"

"Okay, hon. Be careful. I'll be leaving shortly. I'll pick up the stuff on the way home He noticed that some people were putting on their coats and heading home. Since his contacts were finished for the day, he decided to check out and leave before the snow got too heavy.

As he approached his car, he took out his wallet but found only a buck. He would have to stop at the ATM on the way home. When he pulled up to the bank, he walked to the ATM machine. A large sign said that the machines were out of order and he would have to go inside.

Ray noticed the security guard as he entered the bank. There were only six customers. One of the four tellers was waiting on a woman with two small children. The other tellers were attending to the remaining customers. The offices adjoining the lobby were empty. Ray guessed that the bigwigs had gone home early.

He was in line when two masked men entered with guns.

"Everyone on the floor,"

The bandits thought this was a perfect time to rob a bank. The police would be busy with traffic accidents, and response times would be delayed.

One of the bandits went up to the security guard and struck him in the head with the butt of his rifle. The guard went down as the bandit kicked his weapon to the edge of the wall.

The bandits shot and wounded a man as he tried to run for the entrance. The woman screamed as she protected her young children. The frightened children began to cry.

The second gunman jumped the counter. "Give me all your money," he demanded.

The tellers complied and emptied their cash drawers. The gunmen wore waterproof jackets with hoods that covered most of their faces. Goggles covered their eyes. One carried a semiautomatic pistol, and the other had an assault rifle.

They were an unusual combination. The bandit carrying the rifle was almost seven feet tall. His partner was close to five foot three. It was impossible to identify their body type because of their heavy jackets.

Ray was on the floor with other customers. He had a weapon, but the bandits were not aware he was armed. He was waiting for an opportunity to end this nightmare. It was a dangerous situation, and Ray knew it. He thought of Lori, their families, and the future. The bandits might kill everyone in the bank. Ray's training took over—he remained calm and waited for the right moment.

The bandit behind the counter gathered the money in a bag. He jumped over the counter and slipped. Everything scattered as the bandits watched the money spill on the floor. Ray took out his weapon and fired, striking the bandit's shoulder and causing his weapon to drop to the floor.

The second gunman fired at Ray, but missed, shattering the clock on the wall. Ray fired again and wounded the second bandit. He dropped the rifle in excruciating pain.

"Stay away from those weapons," Ray ordered as he pointed his weapon at the bandits.

At that moment, the police rushed through the door. Pointing their weapons at Ray, they told him to drop his weapon. Ray complied with the request.

One of the tellers had pushed her robbery button and notified the police. The security officer told the police what had unfolded during the robbery.

EMTs arrived and started to treat the wounds of the victims and bandits. Further treatment continued at the hospital under police escort. The police examined Ray's credentials.

When they discovered his status and background, they returned his weapon and thanked him for his involvement. Ray was free to leave. He agreed to submit a statement through his office.

In the blizzard, driving was a challenge. The snowplows were barely keeping up. He still had only a buck in his wallet, but he found another bank closer to home.

This time, the ATM had no problem dispensing the few bucks needed to buy Lori's groceries. Luckily, the corner supermarket was still open.

Bread, milk, and sandwich meat arrived home with Ray. Lori gave him a kiss when he entered.

"Looks like you made it safe and sound," he said.

"There were a few anxious moments, but I survived," Lori said.

"Anything happen to you?"

"Nope, nothing. Let's eat."

Chapter 12

The next morning, the snowstorm was over. The snowplows had been busy all night clearing the roadways. For the most part, the streets were passable.

The sun was shining, but it was below freezing.

Ray did not jog, because snow was blocking the sidewalks. He got himself another coffee as Lori left for work. He looked out his living room window and noticed how the street below looked magical after a snowstorm. After a few days, the dirt covering the snow was no longer attractive.

When Ray arrived at the office, most of his colleagues were already there. Keeping the roads clear allowed most people to get to work. He noticed a memo on his desk from his boss. The memo instructed all members of his group to report to the meeting room in ten minutes.

A crowd of people had already assembled when Betty joined the group. There were about eighty-five people. The early arrivals sat at the conference table while others were standing along the walls. The room chatter quieted down when Bob entered the room.

"Hi, everyone, glad you could make it," said Bob. "As most of you know, we got a new director several months ago. Since then, the company has undergone some changes. Most of the changes didn't affect our group . . . until now. Shortly our group will be involved in operations which will take place in the Pacific Northwest. These projects are permanent. The Washington location is counterproductive to our mission. Therefore, our group is moving to Anchorage, Alaska—permanently."

There was a gasp heard though out the room.

"I know this is coming as a surprise to most everyone. We will do everything we can to accommodate you, and we know this move could be a hardship for your families. If you have enough time in service to retire, we will do everything to assist you. If you elect to leave the group or transfer to another agency, it will not go against your record.

"My wife and I plan for early retirement and are leaving next month for Florida. Russ Cunningham is taking over my position in Anchorage. I know you have many questions. A booklet is being prepared and will be available shortly. It should answer most of your concerns, as we expect to complete the move in six weeks. I'll be in my office. If you need to see me, just call Betty Jordan for an appointment. It was a pleasure working with all of you—good luck in whatever you decide. Thank you all."

Everyone followed Bob out of the room and returned to their regular work areas.

Ray went down to the cafeteria and ordered a tuna fish sandwich and a small carton of milk. He paid for his meal and looked around for an empty table. When he was not on assignment, he usually had lunch with Jim. Bill and Ed were sitting at a table in the far corner of the cafeteria.

Ray walked up to the table and asked, "Who is minding the gate?"

Ed was quick to answer, "We have a couple of chimps who take over when we go on break. Have a seat."

Ray smiled as he placed his tray on the table and sat down. He took a bite out of his sandwich.

Bill asked, "Are you going to Anchorage?"

Ray said, "How do you know about that?"

"We're security—we know everything."

"This all came as a surprise," said Ray. "I know my wife will be hostile to it. She already hates the little snow we have here in

Washington. Can you imagine how she will feel in Alaska? She wants to go back to Florida. I have to go home tonight to tell her."

"I met your wife a couple of times. I wouldn't want to tell her either," added Bill. "I'll tell you what, my uncle is a captain on the Polk County sheriff's department. Maybe they can find something for you there."

"Polk County? That's where Lakeland is located. Lori would love it. Wait—I don't think she would like me riding around in a cruiser, although I wouldn't mind it."

"I think your qualifications are in the investigative end. I'll call my uncle tonight—maybe they have something."

Chapter 13

R ay was not looking forward to telling Lori about the Anchorage
move. He rehearsed all the way home in an effort to ease Lori's
pain.

When Ray walked into the apartment, she said, "I already know
about Anchorage."

"How did you find out?"

"Chris Cunningham was so excited about moving to Anchorage,
she couldn't wait to tell me. She thought that you had already
phoned from the office and . . . I don't want to move to Alaska! All
the problems when we were in college. I loved the snow when I saw
it for the first time. The snowball fights and building snowmen. We
had a great time. Soon, it was not fun anymore. The cold, scraping
the windshield, frozen gas lines, traffic, and always being late for
classes. I had three fender-benders because of the icy roads. Battery
and radiator problems, the list goes on. One week, we got hit with
three snowstorms."

After Lori was finished, there was a short pause.

"Maybe I can get out of going to Alaska," said Ray. "Bill Arnold,
remember him? His uncle is a captain in a sheriff's office. He's going
to find out if there's a job for me."

"So where is this sheriff's office? Out in the boondocks?"

"Polk County."

Lori's eyes widened. She rushed over and gave him a kiss and a
hug.

"That's great."

"Wait a minute, babe. I don't have the job yet."

"Let's make sure we say our prayers tonight."

The next morning, Ray pulled up to the stop bar leading into the parking garage. He already had his badge clipped to his shirt. He did not want to get on Bill's bad side.

Ed was operating the gate.

"Hi, Ed. Where's Bill?"

"He's in the security office. He would like to see you."

"Okay," Ray said as the stop bar lifted.

The security office was on the first floor next to the front entrance. Benny was sitting on a stool.

"Benny, I normally see you on the third floor. Did you get a promotion?"

Benny did not say a word as he motioned Ray to enter the security office. Bill was sitting at the front desk. The back door was open, and dozens of monitors were flickering in the background.

Bill pulled over a chair for Ray. "I called my uncle last night, but he wasn't home. Ray, you must lead a charmed life because my aunt told me he was here in Washington reporting to a congressional committee about some crime statistics. Anyway, I called him on his cell phone. I told him your situation. He would like to meet you and Lori at the Capital Grill at seven. Can you make it?"

"Sure."

"Is your resume updated?"

"I'll update it today."

"Who do I ask for when I get to the restaurant?"

"Eddy Arnold."

Lori and Ray arrived at the restaurant at 6:55. Ray was in his best business suit, and Lori wore her favorite green dress and matching shoes.

"Eddy Arnold?" asked Ray as he approached the maître d'. He looked at his floor map and said, "Follow me, please."

Lori and Ray were taken to a table where a man around fifty-five was seated. He rose when he saw them approaching. He said, "Hi, I'm Captain Eddy Arnold—not the singer."

Ray introduced Lori and himself.

The captain began, "Bill has told me about your move to Alaska. We have openings for three investigators. Some of our people are in Afghanistan on military reserve active duty. We are a little shorthanded."

"What happens when they return?"

"Our budget is solid. There is room for the returning military people—plus anyone we hire."

"I'm really interested in joining your department. My wife wants to return to Florida—most of her family still lives there."

"I retired from NCIS after twenty years. I have been with sheriff's office for eight years.

"Did you bring a resume?"

Ray handed the captain his resume.

"When I get back to Florida, we'll take a good look at your qualifications. The sheriff, human resources, and command officers will have a say. We should give you an answer in a couple of days. I'm flying back to Orlando tonight."

"Can I come with you?" asked Lori.

They all smiled.

Chapter 14

One day, two days, three days—still the sheriff's office failed to call. Bill Arnold would ask every day if anyone had called.

"No, not yet," Ray would answer.

Lori would call as well but still the answer was "Not yet."

A few of Ray's colleagues had left the company for other agencies, but most of the group was preparing for Alaska. Some of the cubicles were vacant as the advance group departed to Anchorage.

The days were long as Ray waited. Staying busy was difficult.

On a dreary Saturday, Lori and Ray had nothing planned. He loved to golf, but his interests were on other matters. They were relaxing and hoping for a phone call from Polk County. Ray, with coffee in his hand, was looking out the window and noticed a moving truck had pulled up to the curb across the street. He saw Russ and Chris Cunningham come out and talk to the moving people. Shortly, they began loading furniture and household items.

Ray went to the sofa and read the morning paper. Lori was puttering around. in the kitchen. Four hours later, their doorbell rang. Lori invited Russ and Chris inside.

"Well, we're packed and ready to go," Chris announced. "The truck is loaded and we're on our way. We'll miss you guys." With tears in her eyes, she rushed over to Lori and gave her a hug.

Ray rose, shook Russ's hand, and said, "We'll miss you guys too." They watched teary eyed as Chris and Russ left. The weekend ended with no calls from the sheriff's office.

Back at work, Ray noticed a few more empty cubicles. It was getting lonely in his work area. He was checking his e-mail when a female hand tapped him on his shoulder.

"Hi, Ray," said Barbara. "Today is my last day, and I wanted to say good-bye; I decided to go home to Alabama.

"Good luck, Barbara," Ray said and kissed her on the cheek.

He returned to his e-mail.

Betty Jordan called and said, "Ray, if you got a minute, can you come up to Mr. Miller's office?"

"Sure, I'll be right up."

Ray figured that Bob Miller was about to give him his Anchorage instructions. Once Ray got his schedule, Lori would give her notice at the academy and they would start packing.

"Go right in, Ray. He's waiting for you."

Bob Miller was seated and waiting.

"How you doing, Ray?"

"Fine, Mr., Miller."

"You know, since we're going to be neighbors, you can call me Bob."

"I don't understand."

"You got the job with the Polk County sheriff's office."

"That's great!"

"Since I'll be in Tampa, we'll be neighbors. We've known about your application since day one. They are sorry it took so long, but they had to be thorough. Until you learn the ropes, they will assign you to the homicide division as a trainee. I take it you will accept the position?"

"Oh yes," Ray said.

"Fine. Captain Arnold will call tonight and welcome you aboard. Congratulations. I know you will do a great job."

Ray could not wait to tell Lori.

Bob said, "Call your wife. I'm sure she would like to know. Use my phone."

Ray dialed Lori's number. When she answered, he said, "Give your notice, honey. We're going to Florida."

Chapter 15

Ray finished his last day with the company. They expected him to start his new job in two weeks. He said his good-byes to his colleagues, including Bill Arnold.

Moving and packing was always a challenge. Ray was home alone packing knickknacks, pictures, and items they barely used. The college girls down the hall gave Ray the much-needed boxes. Lori still had a few days before she finished at the academy.

Ray noticed the footlocker in the bedroom closet. He removed the case and placed it on the coffee table. He opened the cover. A purple cloth hid its contents. Ray removed the cloth to expose the Veracruz. He picked up the Veracruz and placed it in on a clear space on the table. He pushed the star to operate the compartment and to exposed the filler hole. He picked up the Olmec potion bottle. Carefully he removed the top and placed his nose near the opening. The fragrance reminded him of gardenias. He replaced the top and put the bottle on the table. Humankind's creations failed to produce anything near the incredible exhibition of the Veracruz. Ray tried to visualize the intellect required to produce such a contrivance. He realized that the Veracruz had unlimited powers and it was up to him not to abuse Paco's trust. Paco's instructions had been very clear.

Ray wanted to witness more of its powers. He could go back in time—hundreds of years if he wanted. He could see major historic events, observe crimes, or expose the truth, but he decided to try something different.

He set the rings to 1863. Knowing that the Olmec potion was at a premium, he placed two drops into the filler hole. He noted the time on his wristwatch, but did not put his finger on the medallion.

Soon everything was a mist. The mist turned into a slight breeze. The curtains waved as they reacted to the draft. When the mist cleared, the Veracruz had vanished. Everything, other than the Veracruz disappearance, remained the same.

He heard the sickening sound of brakes squealing. He ran to the living room window. A little girl was in the road. He rushed down three flights of stairs.

When he got outside, she was sitting up and crying. She looked about seven or eight. He quickly examined her and found that the worst of her injuries was a skinned knee.

A slow moving postal jeep had struck her. The driver was a little distraught, but Ray assured him that she looked okay. The squealing noise came from a different car traveling in the left lane reacting to the child being struck. The postal truck had barely touched her.

Just then, several police cruisers arrived. The officers rushed over to see how the girl was doing.

From the apartment across the street, a woman rushed to the girl's side.

"Mommy, mommy."

"Becky, what happened?"

"I was walking Muffin when she saw another dog across the street. She ran and I followed, but I did not look when I crossed . . . I'm sorry, Mommy."

"That's okay." Her mother gave her a hug.

Muffin remained at her side while the paramedics examined her thoroughly. Her injuries were minor, but they wanted to take her to the hospital as a precaution. Her mother agreed.

Becky and her mother thanked Ray. They started for the hospital but stopped soon. The door opened as Muffin jumped in. After giving the police his account, Ray returned to his apartment.

It had been almost an hour since Ray initiated the Veracruz sequence. He got a glass of milk and sat down. Without warning, the breeze quieted as a mist developed. The mist got thicker and then began to clear. Everything was the same except the Veracruz had reappeared.

Several days later, Lori had finished at the academy. She had said her good-byes to the people she worked with. Her old car needed some bodywork and taking it to Florida would be a risk. One of her students had made her a good offer.

Lori's father had rental property near Lakeland, and he offered it to Ray and Lori. She had relatives and close friends in the quiet community.

Chapter 15

The home was a Craftsman-style bungalow with three bedrooms, a double garage, and modern appliances. All the interior rooms were recently painted.

It had a Lanai with an outdoor area covered with pavers and a fireplace equipped for barbeques.

Lori's father and sister arrived to lend a hand. After several hours under Lori's direction, it was starting to get a little frustrating, but Ray knew if his wife was not happy, no one was happy.

Later that evening, Ray sent out for pizza. During a quiet moment while they were enjoying their pizza, Lori said, "I'm pregnant!"

Everyone stopped eating and rushed to congratulate her.

"Ray, I wanted to tell you earlier, but it wasn't the right time or place. I'm so happy to be here."

By the next day, most of the moving chores had been completed. Ray got up and made coffee. It was okay, but not like Hugo's. While he was making toast, Lori entered the kitchen dressed in one of her best suits.

"Where are you off to? " he asked.

"I have a job interview."

"With whom?"

"I'll tell you if I get the job," she said playfully. "I'm taking your car; can you stay busy while I'm gone?"

"I'll be okay. I'm going to scope out our new neighborhood."

His new neighborhood had gracious homes with well-maintained lawns and landscapes. The area had a nice mixture of homes, small farms and orange orchards. As he jogged onto a side road, a small goat blocked his path. Ray stopped as the goat came over and licked his hand. Just then, another little goat started chewing on his running pants.

"Looks like you met Barney and Clyde."

A man about his age was leaning on the fence.

"I guess so," said Ray.

The man hopped the fence and said, "I'm Paul Audette, that's my little homestead over there." He pointed to a ranch style home about fifty yards from the road. "These little guys do nothing but chew all day. Eventually they get out of the yard, and then I have to catch them and take them home."

"I'm Ray Callahan, just moved in on Purple Martin Drive. I'm originally from Boston."

"Small world. I'm from Rhode Island—been here about eleven years. Barney and Clyde are getting a little frisky I have to take them home. Welcome to the neighborhood."

Ray jogged home, took a shower, and put on clean clothes. He was making himself another coffee when Lori walked in.

"How did you make out?"

"They liked my credentials. They did not have a problem with my pregnancy. If I pass the physical, then the job is mine."

"When you going for your physical?"

"I already did—and I passed. I was so sure we would come to Florida, I had the physical in Washington and had the results sent to the Polk County School District. I start April 1."

"Lori, you never fail to amaze me. Let's eat."

After lunch, Lori and Ray drove around to get a feel for their new surroundings. They visited several auto dealerships to find a new car for Lori.

Lori and Ray were in the local supermarket when Lori asked Ray about the case.

"What case?"

"You know what case I'm talking about—don't act innocent."

"Lori, this is not the time or place to discuss the case. We'll talk about it when we get home."

"Okay," said Lori.

With the shopping finished, Ray unloaded the car while Lori put the groceries away. When they finished, Lori asked, "Ready to talk about the case?"

"Inside the case is a gift given to me by the people who I helped during my last assignment. They mentioned that the gift is a secret and not to tell anyone. When I returned to Washington, I was surprised that you did not ask about the case or its contents. You could not open the case because I had the only key. I knew you would eventually ask, and I was trying to come up with a tale to tell you. When I thought about it, I knew you would keep the secret—and I decided to tell you the truth."

Ray went and got the case and set it on the table. Lori watched intently. Ray placed the key into the lock and lifted the cover. He removed the purple cloth and pointed to the object.

"Lori, this is called a Veracruz. The Veracruz will allow you to travel back in time."

Lori looked as if she was not sure whether to believe him.

"The five rings are used to set the time and date you want to travel back to."

Ray pushed the star. The compartment drawer came out and exposed the bottle. He explained how the Veracruz worked and the three rules.

"Wow," exclaimed Lori. "Who made this?"

"Can't tell you—because no one actually knows. Lori, this is very important. Do not tell anyone about the Veracruz—no one—including your parents and sister. If someone wants to know what's in the case, just tell them it's Ray's junk and let it go at that."

"Have you used it?"

"I've used it twice. Once to feel the effect and then as an experiment. It was a great experience"

"I want to try it too!"

"You can't."

"Why not?"

"Because you're pregnant—it may harm the baby."

"You're right. Maybe we can discuss it more after the baby comes. However, I want to know if you had any adverse effects after you used it."

He assured her that he had no adverse effects that he knew of. It left Lori cautiously feeling better.

Chapter 16

On the first day at their new jobs, Ray was up early. He felt good after a workout.

"A little nervous?" asked Lori as she finished dressing.

"I'm a little curious as to what to expect—not nervous. The first day on a new job, you never know."

Ray pulled into the sheriff's office building. Police cruisers were pulling in and out of the parking area as shifts were changing. A sergeant was handling the front counter.

"Hi, I'm Ray Callahan. This is my first day."

The sergeant put out his hand and said, "Welcome. I'm Aubrey Willis. We've been waiting for you. Have a seat—someone will be out here shortly."

"Hi, I'm Peggy Boule, sheriff's human resources department. I'm here to get you started.

Peggy was tall for a woman, almost six feet. She had a thin figure and a soft face that was pleasant to look at. It seemed that human resources always got the best-looking women.

Peggy brought Ray to an area boxed off by cubicles.

"This is where you'll be working."

Ray noticed a solid mahogany desk, three phones, computer and filing cabinets. A nameplate "Raymond Callahan, Investigator" brought a smile to his face.

"Come, we have more to see," she said as she brought him to a large office with a great view. Peggy looked into the office and addressed the man sitting behind the desk. "Are you busy?"

He looked up and replied, "No, come right in."

"Ray, this is Captain Kenneth Leahey. He's the commander of the group you'll be assigned to."

"Welcome, Ray." Captain Leahey shook his hand.

Peggy continued, "You'll be seeing a lot more of Captain Leahey in the future, but first we'll have to go to my office to finish some paperwork."

Ray was a trainee and would have a training officer help him over the rough spots.

When Peggy took Ray back to his new office, an African-American female was waiting for them.

Peggy said, "Ray, this is Toni Lima. She is going to be your training officer."

"Hi," she said. "Welcome to our group."

Ray, a little puzzled, extended his hand to return her handshake. Peggy excused herself.

Toni asked Ray about his homicide experience.

"Not very much," said Ray.

"I read your jacket and I think you'll fit in nicely. How are your computer skills?"

"Not bad. Between college and Washington, I've been exposed to most computer programs."

Toni went through the passwords on his computer. She tutored him on office procedures, state, and federal laws. Ray had confidence he could remember all of Toni's information.

After a quick lunch, Toni continued from where she left off. Ray was impressed with Toni's knowledge and intellect.

Toni handed Ray some pamphlets, booklets, and paperwork.

"Read these. It will help you do your job better. It is almost six. Congratulations—you survived your first day. Go home!"

When Ray got home, Lori was cooking supper. "How did it go today?"

"Not bad. I learned a lot, and I'm impressed with the department. How about you?"

"My day was fantastic. Everything was perfect. I enjoyed every aspect of the school. I finished my day, and when I went out to the parking lot, I noticed that my front tire was flat. I called the dealership and explained my situation. A man showed up with a new tire and rim. I was on my way in less than ten minutes."

Chapter 17

Ray's training schedule was progressing thanks to Toni's tutoring. He investigated several crimes under Toni's watchful eye. He explored the crimes like a seasoned professional. If he made a mistake, Toni pointed out his error and rectified it. His evaluation reports were favorable, and he was a natural for police work.

Personnel removed Ray's trainee status after three months, and he became a qualified homicide investigator. His new partner was Toni Lima.

Lori did not have any problem with Ray working with a female. She trusted him and her husband, Frank, was a big guy—a really big guy.

Lori was well along in her pregnancy. Ray was concerned that she may be working too hard and wanted her to slow down. She assured him that she was fine and wanted to have Thanksgiving dinner at their house. He reluctantly agreed—providing she took it easy.

Ray invited Bill Arnold, who was in town visiting his uncle. They also invited Captain Arnold and his wife. Her parents and sister, Susan, were included.

Susan was attending college in Tampa and wanted to invite her boyfriend. "The more the merrier," Lori said.

Lori had plenty of help cooking the turkey and all its fixings. Their dining room could easily accommodate the nine people at the dinner table. Her mother brought her best china, serving utensils, and table linens. The dinner looked like it came out of a Norman

Rockwell painting. Lori spent most of the day with a big smile on her face. Everything was perfect.

After the meal, the men watched a few football games and got to know each other. The women tended to business in the kitchen. The men offered to help, but the women wanted them to relax.

Ray said, "If it wasn't for Bill, we would be eating moose in Alaska."

They all laughed and toasted Bill.

*   *   *

Ray was finishing paperwork from a previous case when Captain Leahey asked to meet him in his office.

Leahey said, "I guess you know that Toni is undergoing minor knee surgery today and should join us tomorrow. This is something that she has been putting off. She was in a lot of pain and decided to have the surgery. If all goes well, she should be back tomorrow."

"Toni mentioned the surgery and told me it's no big deal. She's a strong woman and shouldn't have any problems."

"Ray, I know you and Toni normally work homicide cases, but I have to change your current assignment and concentrate on a case that occurred last night. I have most of our group working on this problem. Last night, the daughter of Steven Bibeau was kidnapped. They found her car in a busy parking area at the Florida Southern College campus. This morning, her father got a call from the kidnappers demanding one million dollars. If he notified the police, they would kill her. They added they were watching him. His New York offices were the people who called our sheriff. The kidnappers told him to wait for further instructions."

Steven Bibeau owned a successful dairy business with a large herd of Guernsey and Black Angus cattle. It had lucrative contacts with Florida school districts, supermarkets, and cruise lines. Most of his income came from his publishing business in New York City. Raising a million dollars would not be problem. He was a snowbird and possessed large estates in New York and Florida.

The captain continued, "His daughter was a student at Florida Southern College. We know it happened around 8:15 last night according to her friend. Ginny Ricci told us that Angela had dropped her off at her dormitory around eight. She tried to call her cell phone a couple of hours later, but she failed to get an answer. Another friend at Angela's sorority confirmed that she and her car were not there. Angela had an important exam the next morning and wanted to get home to study. After several hours, Ginny sensed something was wrong and called campus police. They checked the area then notified the sheriff's office.

"Eventually the campus police found the car abandoned in a busy parking area on campus. They checked the surrounding buildings, but found nothing. We towed the car to our garage. CSI examined the car and found fingerprints, hair follicles, and hamburger wrappers. Most of the prints are from Miss Bibeau and her friends. The hair evidence investigation is inconclusive.

"They checked the cameras on campus. Unfortunately, the camera at the parking lot malfunctioned. Some of my investigators are talking to Ginny, other friends, and Mr. Bibeau. CSI has finished with the car. I'd like you to go over to the impound yard—maybe you can spot something that was overlooked. More likely, you wouldn't find anything. CSI does a fantastic job, but we want to solve this thing before the girl is harmed."

"I'm on my way," said Ray as he departed the captain's office.

Chapter 18

On his way to the impound yard, he stopped at his house for several minutes. Lori was still at work.

It was starting to get cloudy as Ray arrived at the impound yard. He introduced himself to Pat Noonan, the yard supervisor. He informed Ray that he could find the Dodge Stratus parked in the far corner of the yard.

"What's in the duffel bag?"

"Just some instruments," Ray said.

"If you need any help, just whistle."

"Okay, I'll be a while—an hour or so—I've got a lot of work."

Ray walked to the far side of the yard. He looked around and could barely see Pat's office. He opened the doors and sat in the backseat. There were signs that CSI had probed the car for evidence.

He took the Veracruz out of the duffel bag and placed it on his lap. The rings were set to seven fifty—last night, just before the abduction.

Normally the Veracruz and the person with a finger on the silver medallion would return to the past, but any component of an item could also return to the past if was placed on the silver medallion. The seatbelt was part of the car.

He pushed the diamond star as the compartment with the bottle slid from the Veracruz.

He placed an edge of the seatbelt and his finger on the silver medallion. The mist appeared and covered the interior.

The car remained, since any covered conveyance will remain intact as past events unfold. Using the Veracruz inside a moving vehicle instead of remaining at a fixed location was a new development. He wondered if the Mayans were aware of this. This would work on a train, airplane, or flying silver clouds. This was a great discovery.

As the mist cleared, the Stratus was traveling the highway. Two females were in the front seats—Angela was driving.

Ginny said, "You're really concerned about your exam tomorrow. Do you think you'll pass?"

"I think I'll do okay, but I've got to study tonight. My father will be disappointed if I don't do well."

Gin "Well, good luck. I'll call later.

They arrived at her dormitory.

Angela and Ginny had been friends since they were youngsters. They came from affluent families on New York's Upper East Side.

Ginny was on the short side and a little plump. She had mid-length red hair and a face full of freckles. She was well-liked, a good student, and lived in one of the college's dormitories.

Angela was blonde and extremely good looking. She could have been a fashion model or spokesperson. She was tall and turned heads when she entered a room. Her many friends included boys. She wanted to concentrate on her studies and did not want a steady beau. She got her good looks from her father and Polish-born mother. Although her family was wealthy, she was careful with money.

Her major was architecture and could have gone to most colleges in the country. She chose Florida Southern College because of the Frank Lloyd Wright influence and the great reputation of the college. Her sorority was several blocks away from Ginny's dormitory.

"Okay, good luck tomorrow."

Ginny closed the door and departed the vehicle.

Angela arrived at the parking lot in front of her sorority building. She was about to get out when a masked gunman ordered her back into the car.

"If you scream, I will kill you. Now drive—I will tell you where to go."

"Please do not kill me. I'll do whatever you ask."

She drove out the parking lot and left the campus. The gunman wore a black leather jacket and black gloves. He ordered her to drive to a location twelve miles away. They pulled up to a parking lot of a pizza parlor. A few customers were inside.

There were four other cars in the lot, but there were no people around.

There was a beat-up rolled awning above the stores front window. There was an apartment above the store with darkened windows. A neon sign with a few missing letters buzzed, dimmed, and then flashed again. The kidnapper pointed to a door on the left side of the entrance to the pizza parlor.

"When I tell you, walk to that door and open it. I will be right behind you. Do not run away or I will gun you down like a dog. Walk up the flight of stairs to the second floor."

The gunman held the hidden weapon to her side. She opened the door and they walked upstairs. Ten minutes later, the gunman returned alone. He drove to the campus and parked. He walked to a motorcycle at the rear of the building, put on his helmet, and sped away.

The sheriff's office was a beehive of activity.

A deputy assigned to the front desk rushed into Captain Leahey's office and said, "Captain, I just got an anonymous call from a person who knows where the Bibeau girl is being held."

"What?"

"The call came from a pay phone, but I didn't recognize the voice. The caller reported the girl was above a pizza parlor at 9257 Greenwood Road. He said to hurry because the girl may be killed."

"Okay, alert SWAT and get over there. We don't have many leads—but we have to move fast if we want to save the girl."

It did not take long for SWAT to surround the pizza parlor and rescue Angela. She was found unharmed, duct taped and tied to a chair. The kidnappers were not in the apartment.

When the excitement was over, SWAT was getting ready to clear the scene. A Harley approached. The biker noticed the police presence and performed a U-turn, accelerating to a high speed. A deputy observed the erratic behavior and gave chase. He radioed other officers who lagged behind, but joined the pursuit.

The chase continued through interstate highways and residential areas. The bike roared through stop signs and traffic lights. He endangered many innocent lives. A single cruiser kept pace. He radioed his position to his fellow officers.

The bike was cornered in a cul-de-sac. He stopped and opened fire on the officer. One of his bullets found their mark and the officer fell to the ground.

The Harley screamed out of the cul-de-sac as the cruisers continued the pursuit. The Harley was fast, but the cruisers tried to keep up.

The Ultra could reach speeds of over a hundred miles per hour.

Chapter 19

Lights were flashing as the stop gate came down at a railroad crossing. Several vehicles were already stopped. The biker roared down the road followed by four sheriff's cruisers with sirens blaring and flashing lights warning of possible danger.

The motorcycle went around the parked cars and crashed through the stop gate. As he went over the tracks, a CSX diesel locomotive was passing at the same time. Sparks, debris, and dust scattered along the tracks. It was a mile before the freight train was able to stop. The cyclist died instantly

In the side bags, they found the million-dollar ransom. Sheriff's deputies identified Michael Wiley as the biker. Steven Bibeau had hired him as an accountant several years earlier. Fired for embezzlement—and after a fourteen-month stay in prison—Michael fell on hard times. He blamed the Bibeau family for his bad luck and wanted revenge. He was the lone kidnapper.

The sheriff shot by Wiley survived and returned to duty eight weeks later.

When Ray arrived home, Lori had dinner waiting for him. He kissed his wife and went into the bathroom to wash his hands. They were eager to eat the pork chops, mashed potatoes, and peas Lori had prepared.

"Were you involved with the kidnapping case I've been hearing about all day on TV?"

"The department put all its resources on the case and I'm one of the resources."

"Did you use the Veracruz?"

"Yes, I did—and I discovered something very interesting. You have to be intelligent to understand what I'm about to tell you."

"Ray, I'm a college graduate."

"Okay, see if you can follow. When we used the Veracruz to go back in time, we remained at the same location, but at an earlier time. Got it?"

"Got it. Go on."

"What if you wanted to change locations while in a car, train, or plane? Placing part of the covered conveyance on the silver medallion along with your finger allows the conveyance to remain visible. You can observe everything that transpires inside the vehicle. I used the seatbelt from the car and got the desired results. Do you understand?"

"I think I do. If you used a bicycle or escalator, it would not work, right?"

"Right."

"A canoe wouldn't work, but a cabin cruiser would work because it's covered."

"By God, I think you've got it."

"Ray, after the baby is born, we can take some interesting trips together."

"Honey, I like the way you think."

$$* \quad * \quad *$$

The next morning, Ray was finishing his paperwork from the kidnapping case. Tina was standing in the hallway. He welcomed her back with a hug.

"Looks like your ordeal was a success. You look good and no crutches."

She smiled. She had a bandage on her left knee, but was able to walk without a limp.

"I was in a lot of pain with the swelling, and it was starting to become a problem. I'm glad I listened to you and the captain and had this taken care of.

"I'm glad everything went well. Glad you're back."

"What's going on today?" asked Tina.

"The captain wants us to resume our normal duties."

"Okay, I'm ready to go!"

They returned to their normal duties within the department. By mid–morning, the screaming sounds of fire engines filled the air. A yellow and white flame with black smoke was bellowing out of a vacant motel.

Twelve units were engulfed as was the office in the center of the structure. Two fire trucks were on the scene. The firefighters raced frantically to get the fire under control. More and more men and equipment joined them to battle the blaze, but the flames grew higher. To the side of the motel were a vacant lot, a gas station, and a convenience store. A citrus plant was located a quarter-mile away.

Due to the efficiency of the firefighters, they quickly brought the blaze under control. The structure was still smoldering when they entered the building. Within moments, they carried a body out of the building.

*   *   *

Ray and Tina were finishing lunch when Captain Leahey summoned them to his office.

He said, "This morning there was a motel fire in Lake Wales. It happened on Route 60 just outside the city limits. The motel should have been vacant, but they pulled an unconscious victim out of the ruins. He died at the hospital and is now at the medical examiner's office.

"A preliminary examination indicated that the man died of blunt force trauma and not from the fire. I want you to work jointly with the state fire marshal's office to investigate this case. The fire marshals suspect arson and will investigate the fire aspect. I want you two to concentrate on the homicide.

"I will schedule a meeting with the fire marshal tomorrow morning at nine o'clock. They should have more information by then. Meanwhile, you can visit the fire scene and see what you can uncover. That's about all I have—good luck."

Chapter 20

When Toni and Ray arrived at the fire scene, most of the emergency trucks were gone. They spoke to several firefighters who were checking for flare-ups. They said the victim was still alive when they removed him from the building, but he had died at the hospital. They showed them where CSI had recovered a steel pipe.

Ray and Tina arrived at the state fire marshal's office for their nine o'clock meeting. Lieutenant Frank Williams conducted the meeting. He had joined the state fire marshal's office less than a year earlier.

Frank said, "In order to start a fire, you need three things: oxygen, fuel source, and heat. Our fuel source at the Lake Wales fire was gasoline. The color of the flames told us it was gasoline. Our accelerant detection canines also indicated gasoline. The investigation continues, but we are confident it was arson. Arson is a first-degree felony punishable by up to thirty years in prison.

"The owner of the building is Charles Sonata who is currently on a cruise ship somewhere near Costa Rica. He should return by the weekend, so we will have to wait to question him. Meanwhile, we are looking into his finances, bank accounts, and personal activities. If anything new comes up, we will let you know. Any questions?"

Ray and Toni said, "No" and thanked the lieutenant as they left.

When they got to the parking lot, Ray asked, "Where to next?"

"Medical Examiner's Office," said Toni.

It was a short ride, and Dr. Achinger met them in the examining room. He began to describe his examination, "Our victim was a thirty-six-year-old homeless veteran who had fallen on difficult times. His name was Mathew Cote. Mr. Cote did not die in the fire. Soot was absent from his lungs, and he had several burns not serious enough to cause death. He met his demise when he was struck on the head with a pipe. The outline of the pipe matched the wounds we found on his head. There were several insect bites on his body. The toxicology tests are not back yet, but there was a strong odor of alcohol on his body and clothes.

"Most of the locals knew him as someone seen walking the streets. He would beg for money at the traffic lights or do odd jobs. All his money went to wine and alcohol, and he was intoxicated most of the time. As for drugs, we have been told he never used them. Occasionally he would sleep in the woods or the vacant motel when the police did not run him off.

"Everybody liked him and tried to help by giving him food and clothing, but he was very depressed. He received several medals for heroism in the army. When he returned, he worked at Lowe's as an assistant manager. He has an ex-wife and two sons who live in Lake Wales. I have their address if you want to talk to her."

"Yes," Ray said.

Ray and Toni thanked the doctor, and they left for Lake Wales. Toni called Mrs. Cote to arrange for an appointment to meet with her. Mrs. Cote lived in a very kid-friendly part of town.

Ray and Toni pulled up to the ranch style home as she met them at the door. Her puffy face was youthful, but displayed years of stress. She offered them something to drink, but they declined.

Visibly shaken, she explained the events that had started five years earlier.

"Five years ago, we had three young children: a seven-year-old boy, a five-year-old boy, and a three-year-old daughter, Bunny. It was a struggle in those days. Matt did not make enough money, so I had to work part time to make ends meet. He kept an eye on the kids when I went to work. We had just bought this house and making the mortgage payments and paying other endless bills was a burden.

"One weekend while I was at work, Matt was taking care of the kids. He was trying to fix a leaking toilet and lost track of time. When he finished, he could not locate the kids. Eventually, he found the boys at a neighbor's house, but Bunny was still missing. After a frantic search, they found her lifeless body at a nearby lake.

"After the funeral, Matt blamed himself and cried all night as he started to drink heavily. His drinking only got worse. He was unbearable to live with. He was drunk all the time. Eventually he lost his job, and I filed for divorce and kicked him out of the house.

"He begged me to let him back in, but I refused unless he got help. He still loved the boys and me, but he refused to become sober. I loved him too, but I could not continue with this situation. He never abused me physically, but he begged me to let him come back. I continually refused.

"I could have had him arrested for lack of child support, but I felt sorry for him. Basically, he was a great person and willing to help anyone. Tragically, he did not get help for himself. My family helped me financially, so I was able to keep the house and give my boys a home. Now I have a good job, and my family, friends, and church have been supportive. I'm positive we'll be okay."

"That's wonderful," said Toni. "Do you know anyone who would want to harm your husband?"

"Not really. Everyone liked Matt—I'm not aware of any enemies. There are not many transients in Lake Wales."

Ray said, "I think we have what we are looking for. Thank you for your time, Mrs. Cote. We'll do our best to find the person responsible for your husband's death."

Toni and Ray hugged her as she began to cry. She waved from the door with tears in her eyes as they walked to their car.

Chapter 21

Ray and Toni returned to the fire scene. They spoke to several witnesses, but they were of no value when it came to the homicide.

They were in front of the motel when a mail carrier walked past. They asked if he had seen anything on the day of the fire.

Dan Foley said, "I was walking past the motel when a young adult, in his early twenties, almost hit me. He was riding an orange bicycle. I continued to the convenience store to deliver their mail and got a cup of coffee. As I was enjoying my coffee, I looked out the window and down the street. I could see the motel was on fire. I called the fire department and they were here in a matter of minutes."

"Can you identify the person on the bicycle, Mr. Foley?" asked Tina.

"I think I can." He gave them a full description. They thanked him for his information and returned to their car.

They put the information about the bicycle and rider out on the airways.

It was not long before the Lake Wales city police reported they found an orange bike near the town park. Further investigations revealed that a similar bike had been stolen from the high school that morning. Ray suggested turning the bike over to CSI for evidence.

While reviewing overnight reports, Captain Leahey informed Tina and Ray that Lieutenant Williams was going to interview Charles Sonata later that afternoon.

Ray and Toni met Lieutenant Williams in his office ten minutes before Mr. Sonata arrived. He told them that Sonata's finance and bank accounts were troubling. Friends said he was spending a lot of time at the casino.

Sonata arrived for his two o'clock appointment. He had just finished his Caribbean vacation, and his cruise ship had docked that morning at Port Everglades.

Sonata and his wife were estranged. She was up north, and he lived in a gated community in Mulberry. He owned three dry cleaners across Polk County.

He had acquired the motel several years earlier. The previous owner had neglected the motel so badly—especially the illegal prostitution—that it was a public nuisance and was closed by the local authorities.

Sonata bought the motel at a bargain price and had been informed about the fire while on the cruise.

Williams began, "We are investigating the fire in the motel structure that you own. We extinguished the fire and found the body of a homeless man. We discovered that gasoline was used to start the fire."

"Do you think the homeless man started the fire?" asked Mr. Sonata.

"No, it was not possible for the victim to start the blaze—he was dead before the fire erupted. We found a pipe—the murder weapon—on the floor next to his body."

"If he didn't start the fire, who did?" asked Sonata.

"We don't know, but we are confident it was arson and are aggressively looking for suspects," said Williams.

"I hope you don't believe I had anything to do with this," said Sonata.

"This was not only an arson case, but a homicide as well. Everyone is a suspect," said Williams.

"I wouldn't have a reason to destroy that property. I was in the process of renovating the motel and was prepared to spend a great deal of money. I had a contractor working on the project."

"What's the contractor's name?" asked Williams.

"Dave Josephson. His business is in Lake Wales. Listen, I think I have said enough. Any more questions, call my lawyer. This meeting is over," he said and stormed out of the office.

After Sonata left, Williams said, "Mr. Sonata has something to do with this case. I don't know yet, but time will tell."

They all agreed that the lieutenant would pay a visit to Josephson and Ray and Tina would follow up on the bicycle.

Ray and Tina visited the CSI facility to examine the orange bike. The technician reported there were no viable fingerprints. The only prints were from the officers who had recovered the bike. They asked the mail carrier to identify the bicycle. He arrived several hours later and positively identified it.

"The bike is the key to this case," said Toni.

"You're right," said Ray.

"Let's pay a visit to the high school."

They got permission to talk to the boy who had reported his bike stolen. He was a sixteen-year-old junior named Ricky Wheeler. They found a quiet place in the cafeteria to question him.

Ricky said, "Normally I parked with the other bikes at the bike rack. The school wanted everyone to lock their bikes, and I was no exception. I used a chain wrapped around the bike and then locked it to the rack. When I came out at noon, my bike was gone. Someone used bolt cutters to cut the lock. The only thing remaining was the damaged lock and chain. I called the school security and they notified the police."

"What did you do with the chain and lock?" asked Toni.

"I picked it up by the chain and put the chain and the damaged combination lock into a brown paper bag. I put the bag in my locker near my homeroom."

"Listen very carefully," said Ray, "Do not touch the paper bag. People from the sheriff's office will pick up the bag and give you a receipt. You can wait for them in the principal's office. Thank you, Ricky. You've been a great help."

Toni thanked him as well and they left the school.

As soon as they entered their car, Toni asked CSI to pick up the bag in Ricky's locker.

Ray and Toni were very concerned about the death of Mathew Cote and wanted to solve this mystery for the sake of his family

Ray and Toni looked around the crime scene again, but found nothing of interest.

They decided to walk to the convenience store for something cold to drink. The odor of gasoline was in the air as several motorists were filling their tanks.

As they were paying for their drinks, Ray asked the clerk if she had seen anything the day of the fire.

"I was on duty that day and I remember the fire. Nothing much happens here. Before the fire, a young guy came in carrying a gas container. He said it was for his lawnmower. I thought he was a little strange. He paid for five gallons of gas and I was watching him fill the container. We started to get busy and, when I looked up, he was gone."

"Can you identify him?" asked Toni.

"I'm sure I can," she said.

On their way back to headquarters, Williams called and requested that they meet him at his office.

When they arrived, Williams repeated the conversation he had with Josephson. He acknowledged that Charles Sonata had hired him to do renovations at the motel. Sonata became upset when Josephson told him that the plumbing was bad in every unit and would cost over sixty thousand dollars to correct. At that point, Sonata fired Josephson.

"This is looking more and more like a motive for arson," he said.

Ray and Toni reported on their progress and returned to headquarters to finish the paperwork.

The next morning, Tina and Ray got a call from the technician at CSI. She reported that they gotten a hit from a fingerprint on the combination lock. Ricky Wheeler's prints were on the lock. They lifted another print from the rear plate. They eliminated Ricky's family and friends.

They used the FBI's Integrated Automated Fingerprint Identification System to get a match. The database has more than sixty-six million fingerprints. The data displayed arrest records, crime descriptions, and mugshots.

Chapter 22

The fingerprint belonged to Dale Johnson, a twenty-three-year-old from Fulton, Missouri. They charged him with setting fire to a vehicle, but he had escaped their jurisdiction the day before his trial. They transferred copies of the arrest reports and mugshots to their office.

Captain Leahey suggested they issue a BOLO (Be on the Lookout) for Mr. Johnson. "He is only a person of interest at this point," he concluded.

Toni and Ray left the captain's office, got a copy of the mugshot of Dale Johnson—plus photos of five similar suspects—and traveled to Lake Wales.

After laying out the six photos, the mail carrier and the convenience store clerk each picked out the picture of Dale Johnson as the man they saw the day of the fire. Several days of searching failed to produce the elusive Dale Johnson.

The fire marshals and sheriff's office were at an impasse. There were no records of Dale Johnson.

At the captain's suggestion, they started to interview the dry-cleaning employees.

The first store on the list was at a strip mall in Lakeland. The young male clerk behind the counter had heard of the fire and that someone died there. He said Sonata spent most of his time at the main store in Bartow. They asked him if he knew anyone by the name of Dale Johnson. He didn't.

They showed him the mugshot of Dale Johnson. He said, "That's Don Salter, our delivery truck driver. In fact, he's out back loading his truck."

Ray and Toni went to the back of the store and recognized Dale Johnson. He saw them and ran to the street.

Ray and Tina tried to keep up, but he quickly sped out of sight. They called for backup, and a perimeter was established.

Soon a sheriff's helicopter was overhead. They spotted the suspect a half-mile into the woods. They captured him an hour later after they requested assistance from a K-9 unit.

When they questioned him at headquarters, he denied being at the motel. After several hours of intense interrogation, Ray asked him about the crimes committed in Missouri.

Johnson said, "It all started when I was a teenager. I always liked setting fires; I got a thrill out of it. It made me feel good. In my early teens, my friends and I would set the wheat fields on fire on the way to the movies. We would laugh when the fire trucks passed us on their way to putting out the fire we had just set.

"I was on the baseball team in high school and was considered a good player. I smoked cigarettes after school. The coach was against smoking for his players, and when they caught me, I had to do laps around the field. Well, they removed me from the team when I continued to smoke. When I got the chance, I set the baseball uniforms on fire. They knew it was me, but they could not prove it. I was a hero to some of my friends; it made me feel good.

"When I graduated from high school, I was attending night school to learn the skills needed to become an appliance service man. I was dating a girl that meant a lot to me. I was doing a little crack cocaine, and I got the girl involved as well. Her father found out I was responsible for her addition and forbade me to see his daughter. I poured alcohol in his car and set it on fire as revenge. The police arrested me when a neighbor saw me. I was out on bail, but I left the state before the trial. I came to Florida and changed my name."

"What is your relationship with Mr. Sonata?" asked Ray.

"Mr. Sonata was very good to me. We had long conversations. He wanted me to attend college to get my degree. He also mentioned the motel he bought in Lake Wales. He said that it needed a lot of work and when it was finished, he was going to hire me as the manager. I was very excited."

Toni said, "We know you were at the motel the day of the fire. We have witnesses. Don't lie—we know more than you think we do."

Johnson put his head between his legs. He said, "I was really excited when Mr. Sonata told me he was going to make me the manager. When he told me that the cost of the renovations to the motel was more than he could afford, I became very upset. I wanted revenge."

"What happened next?" asked Ray.

"I thought about it for several days and decided I wanted to hurt Mr. Sonata. I took the truck to the high school. I stole the bike and rode to the motel. I walked over to the convenience store and got gas. I got inside through a broken window, and then poured gasoline around the office and the adjoining units. I was almost finished when this grubby drunk asked what I was doing. He startled me; I didn't know anyone was there. I hit him with a pipe. I started the fire and took off."

"Did you help the man that you struck?" asked Toni.

"No, I panicked and ran. The fire was spreading"

Johnson paused, then put both hands to his face. "I need help. I do not know was wrong with me." He broke down in tears.

They confiscated the truck and found the bolt cutters inside—and then they arrested him.

Chapter 23

A few weeks later, religious displays start appearing on a few desks. The holiday spirit was in the air.

Ray was looking at mugshots when his phone rang.

Captain Leahey said, "Get over to State Road 86 in Citrusville. We are not sure what happened, but there is a dead body inside a burned-out car. Take Toni with you."

As they pulled up to the crime scene, numerous police and fire vehicles dotted the landscape. Carved along the side of the road was a drainage ditch. Fifty feet off the road stood a wire fence. Cows and egrets were grazing on the opposite side.

On the left side were bushes, high grass and woods. Toni and Ray walked up to the smoldering car. They could see the charred remains of a man in the front seat.

Joe Curtin, deputy sheriff, joined them. "I was on patrol when I saw smoke and flames coming from this direction. It was about 1:15. I tried to put out the fire, but the smoke was thick. It was demolished by the time the fire trucks arrived."

A small crowd had gathered. Police interviewed the onlookers but no one had seen the fire start.

Toni said, "Fan out and see what we can find."

Searching failed to produce any evidence. Crime scene technicians took videos, pictures, and 3D scans of the crime scene.

The medical examiners removed the body from the vehicle. A flatbed truck towed the car to the police garage.

Technicians determined that gasoline was the accelerant, but finding fingerprints, DNA, or other evidence was not possible.

The next afternoon, Toni and Ray entered the office of Dr. Allan Achinger.

"What do you have for us?" asked Ray.

"We are still conducting tests, but here's what we have so far. The victim was shot in the left side of the head. We recovered a .38 caliber bullet. There was no evidence of trauma, and toxicology tests were normal. We found four hundred dollars in the victim's wallet. Oliver Duncan lived in Citrusville. He had a wife and a twenty-three-year-old son. My office has notified his family. That's about all we have so far. If we come up with anything new, we'll give you a call."

"Thank you," said Toni.

Ray and Toni discovered that Oliver Duncan had been wealthy and had real estate holdings in most of Florida. He lived on a large ranch in Citrusville with cattle, horses, and citrus groves. He was politically active in the community and did not appear to have any enemies. Most of Duncan's family lived in Alabama. They were questioned about their activities during the time of the murder, but investigators found nothing suspicious.

Twenty-five years earlier, Duncan had come to Florida. He did very well in the citrus business and married a local girl named Judith Wnuk. Their son was active in his father's business.

The victim's wife had been visiting her father at the veteran's hospital in Jacksonville. Her story checked out. Jason, the victim's son, was at a business meeting in New York. They were able to verify his movements.

They questioned his employees, business associates, and friends.

All suspects had a solid alibi. Every interview, record tracking, and bit of research went nowhere. The only evidence was the bullet.

Toni said, "Let's reexamine the evidence. Telephone records indicated Mr. Duncan called his ranch a half hour before his death. Tom Ford, his ranch foreman, said he took the call from Mr. Duncan. Ford claims that Mr. Duncan asked if Lester Fay, the mechanic, had arrived to fix the tractor. He told him that Fay was already there. Mr. Duncan said 'fine' and hung up.

"Fay confirms that he was working on the tractor that day. We asked what Ford was doing all this time. He said he was around, but spent most of his time in the stable."

Every lead turned cold. Questioning friends, relatives, and business associates went nowhere.

Oliver Duncan had been very popular in the community. The news media were putting pressure on the sheriff's department with many calls demanding an arrest. The sheriff and Captain Leahey kept asking for progress reports. The investigative unit was working long hours and getting nowhere.

Ray's wife and Toni's husband complained about the long hours away from home—the pressure on everyone was unbearable. In cases of this type, informants supply crucial information that helps solve many crimes. Not so in this case.

Ray was reluctant to use the Veracruz. The Olmec potion had no refills and he was concerned about the long-term effects on his health. He wanted to rely on his intelligence, training, and police techniques to solve this crime.

Chapter 24

Ray pulled up to the Citrusville crime scene. The charred marking on the side of the road was still visible. He remained in his unmarked car and quietly looked at the landscape.

Deputy Joe Curtin, in his cruiser, pulls up beside him.

"Any luck in the Duncan case?"

"I got a few leads, but nothing so far," said Ray. "We've spent a lot of time on this one."

"So I've heard. This is a lonely road. Not much goes on here," said Joe. "Where's Toni?"

"She's in court testifying before a jury about a case she investigated last year. Did you see anything suspicious the day of the murder?"

"The only thing I saw was the rising smoke through the trees. The road was quiet with no other cars in sight. The nearest residence is four miles down the road."

Both radios came to life. The report was a three-car accident five miles away.

"Good luck—got to go." Joe sped off with his lights flashing.

Ray got out, walked to the rear, and lifted the trunk. Inside was the case. Ray put it on the side of the road and closed the trunk.

He reached into his pocket and used the key to open the cover. He put the Veracruz on the cloth. He set the rings to the date and approximate time of the Duncan murder. He pushed the star and the compartment opened. He removed the Olmec potion and the top. He put one drop into the filler hole.

He replaced the top and returned the bottle to the compartment. He pushed the star as the compartment retracted into the Veracruz. The rings returned to their origin as the silver medallion moved over the filler hole.

He placed his index finger on the silver medallion. When the mist cleared, a car emerged on the edge of the roadway.

Oliver Duncan leaned against his vehicle. A pickup truck driven by his foreman pulled up behind him.

As he got out, he shouted, "I've got your gas."

"Good," said Duncan, "My wife borrowed the car yesterday and failed to fill the tank. Thank God you were at the ranch when I called."

"Pop the filler cover while I add some gas," said Ford.

Duncan got into the front seat and hit the button to open the filler cover. He closed the door and rolled down the window. Instead of putting gas into the tank, Ford moved to the driver's door and fired a weapon through the window.

Duncan died instantly. Ford looked at the smoldering gun. He panicked and ran into the woods. When he found a tree with a decayed opening, he dropped the gun into the tree.

He returned to the car and poured gasoline on the interior. He picked up the shell casing, tossed the gas container inside the car, and then set it on fire.

The vehicle was engulfed as he jumped into his pickup and sped away.

Chapter 25

Early the next morning, Ray juggled two cups of hot coffee as he worked his way to Toni's cubicle. He placed both coffees on her desk.

Toni said, "Didn't sleep too well last night. This case is driving me crazy. My husband says he was going to divorce me if I did not start spending more time at home with him and the kids. He was joking . . . I hope."

Ray sipped his coffee and remained silent.

Toni continued, "All we have is the bullet, no DNA or fingerprints . . . Nada."

"It's a real whodunnit!"

"While you were in court yesterday, I went out to the Citrusville crime scene. I'm sure there's something out there. Let's go back—maybe we missed something."

"We're at a dead end. Okay, let's go back."

They finished their coffees and headed back to Citrusville.

At the Citrusville crime scene, yellow tape was still dancing in the wind.

They repeated the examination of the scene without success. After ten minutes, Ray suggested they try the woods, "Turn over everything—rocks, bushes, and leaves. Maybe something was lost or dropped."

Toni and Ray started to search the woods.

After fifteen minutes, Toni yelled, "Hey, Ray, come over here."

Ray rushed to Toni's side. "What's up?"

"Look at the base of that tree. I turned over all the leaves and debris. Look closely at the decayed bottom of the tree." The handle of a .38 caliber revolver was visible.

"That's it," Ray shouted.

Toni notified CSI and they took pictures of the revolver inside the tree. They retrieved the weapon and documented their findings.

The serial number on the revolver indicated that Tom Ford was the owner. On the weapon, they found his fingerprints. Ballistics tests proved it was the murder weapon. The bullet matched the revolver's characteristic markings. The sheriff's deputies brought Tom Ford in for questioning. He said someone had taken his revolver.

Toni asked, "Why did you not report it stolen? And why are your fingerprints still on the weapon?"

Ford appeared nervous and sweated profusely. Ford finally confessed to the murder of Oliver Duncan. He was having an affair with Duncan's wife.

"Judith Duncan was not involved, in any way," he added.

Ford was arrested and charged with murder. Duncan's wife was never charged. Several years later, he was found guilty of first-degree murder and was sentenced to life imprisonment without the possibility of parole.

Chapter 26

On Christmas Eve, Ray was finishing some paperwork when his phone rang.

Lori said, "Ray, it's time. My parents are here, and they are taking me to the hospital."

"Okay," said Ray. "I'm on my way."

He told Toni that he was on his way to the hospital.

"Good luck," she called out as Ray dashed out of the building.

Ray got on the highway. He had thoughts of rushing to the hospital, but he drove at the speed limit. This was no time to have an accident or hurt someone. This was the night his baby was to be born. He knew Lori would receive the best of care at the hospital.

He entered the hospital garage and found a vacant space close to the main entrance. He walked to the front lobby.

Holiday displays and wishes of glad tidings decorated the lobby. As he waited for the elevator, a volunteer was playing traditional holiday tunes on the grand piano.

A crowd of visitors waited to visit friends and loved ones in the hospital.

As he exited the elevator, he walked down a long hallway. Halfway down the corridor, he noticed a large window that displayed the newest arrivals. Several nurses tended to the infants.

Ray smiled as he found his way to the area where Lori and her parents were waiting. He rushed to her side, and his in-laws joined him.

Lori was in labor, and soon the doctor arrived. A nurse helped Ray put on a hospital gown and mask.

He offered support to Lori as she pushed and breathed and pushed and breathed. After some anxious moments, the baby was born. Soon there was another baby. Lori had given birth to twins, which ran in Ray's family.

The nurses cleaned the babies, and Ray stood in awe, thanking God for both of the perfect babies.

While holding the newborns, he asked, "What do you want to name the babies?"

"Today is Christmas. How about Holly or Carol?"

"Carol it is. What about the boy?"

"It's still Christmas—I like Nicholas. Carol and Nicholas."

"I like that too," Ray said.

Ray decided to go home so that Lori could get some rest. Ray kissed her and told her to get some rest. When he returned, he would be bringing home his wife and babies.

His life was perfect, and he looked forward to many happy years. He was getting comfortable with his job and mastering the Veracruz. He assumed that life would be a lot smoother in the future. On the other hand, will it?

References

The Complete Idiot's Guide To Writing A Novel by Tom Montelelone
Dictionary & Thesaurus by Webster
Book of Facts by Readers Digest
The Scott, Foresman Handbook for Writers by Hairston, Ruszkiewicz, and Friend
Formatting and Submitting Your Manuscript by Chuck Sambuchino
The First Five Pages by Noah Lukeman
Wikipedia: The Free Encyclopedia
The Ledger Newspapers of Lakeland Florida
Polk County Sheriff's Office Website
Florida Division of State Fire Marshal
Myfloridacfo.Com Website
Drug Enforcement Administration (DEA) website
Florida Department of Law Enforcement (FDLE) website
Central Intelligence Agency (CIA) website
Newschief.Com website
FBI-IAFIS
www.fbi.gov website

About the Authors

Peter J. Wetzelaer was born in Providence, Rhode Island, in 1936. He spent most of his early years in Cranston, Rhode Island. He graduated from New England Institute of Technology and has taken courses in electronics, computer science, and software at many universities, including MIT and Northeastern. He was married for forty-four years, had three children, a boy and two girls. Wetzelaer lost his wife to ovarian cancer in 2007.

He married Barbara Johnson on April 2, 2011. His chosen field was electronic technology, and he has designed test equipment and commercial products. He also served as a civilian instructor for the US Navy, teaching about MK-46 torpedoes. His writing experience came from authoring electronic test procedures, equipment descriptions, and instructional documentation. He thought about writing *A Step Back* at the time of the Kennedy assassination. Wetzelaer retired from Bose Corporation after thirty years in 2004. He spends the winter months in Florida and the remainder in Massachusetts.

Barbara A. Johnson was born in Pawtucket, Rhode Island, in 1941. She graduated from Tolman High School in 1959. She moved to California, where she became a manager for Household Finance. She was head of Consumer Credit at Citizens National Bank. In 1978, she returned to Rhode Island and was a life insurance agent for Mass Mutual Life Insurance.

She retired in 2000 after her husband died.

She met Peter J. Wetzelaer in 2008 and married him on April 2, 2011. They split their time between Massachusetts and Florida. She has three sons and nine perfect grandchildren.

The authors have taken six cruises over the last several years. Most of the material for *A Step Back* came from travel experiences. They felt that they had a story to tell and decided to publish a book.